MW01098079

I made this
book for:

_____

Love,

Prudence's Goodnight Book

Prudence's

Goodnight Book

Written and illustrated by Alona Frankel

HarperFestival®

A Division of HarperCollins*Publishers*

To Zygmunt and the lullabyes

Copyright © 1979 by Alona Frankel. Originally published in Israel. First U.S. edition, 2000. Printed in the U.S.A. All rights reserved.
Library of Congress catalog card number: 99-63975
HarperCollins®, ☰®, and HarperFestival® are registered trademarks of HarperCollins Publishers Inc. http://www.harperchildrens.com
"Prudence" is a registered trademark of Alona Frankel. Alona photo: Dina Guna. www.alonafrankel.com

Motto:
Good night, good night
William Shakespeare,
Romeo and Juliet

Hello.
I am Prudence's mother.
I'd like to tell you about Prudence,
and about when, why,
and where Prudence sleeps.
This is Prudence.
Prudence is a little girl.
Little girls need to sleep.
Little girls love to sleep.

From the day Prudence was born she could sleep.
When does Prudence sleep?
When she was a little baby
she slept most of the time, day and night.
She would wake up only when she wanted me, her mother,
to feed her or to change her diaper.
The bigger Prudence grew, the less she slept.
Now Prudence only sleeps at night.

Why does Prudence sleep?
Prudence sleeps because all through the day
she listens, looks, smells, touches, and tastes.
She thinks, learns, plays, laughs, and cries.
She eats, walks, and runs around.
It's all very tiring.
When Prudence is very tired, her eyes close
as if by themselves, and she wants to go to sleep.

Where does Prudence sleep?
Does she sleep in a doghouse?

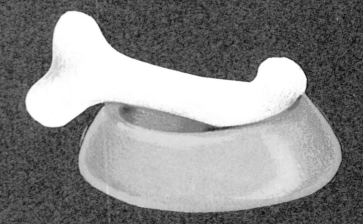

No!
Happy the dog sleeps in the doghouse.

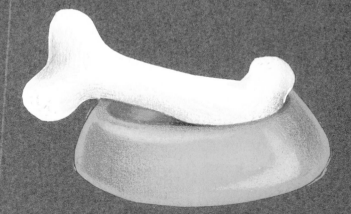

Does she sleep in a nest?

No!
Birds sleep in nests.

Does she sleep under the bed?

No!
Lucifer the cat sleeps under the bed.

Prudence sleeps IN the bed.
What does Prudence
have on her bed?

A mattress,

a bedsheet,

a blanket,

and a pillow.

What does Prudence
have under her pillow?
Prudence's dreams
live under her pillow.

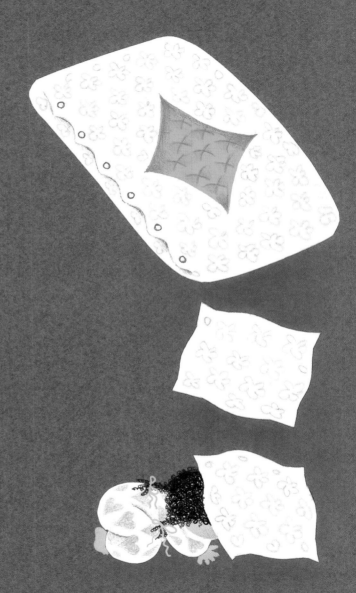

A bed is a marvelous thing!
A bed is a ship that sails into the land of dreams.

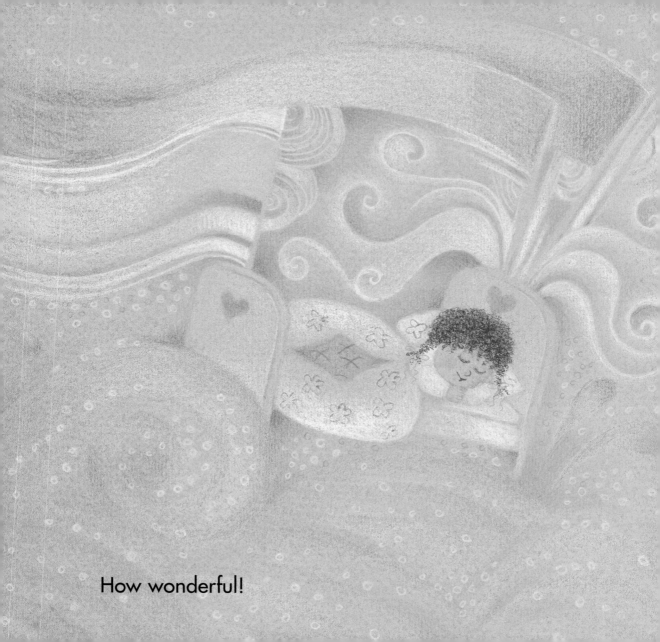

How wonderful!

Dreams.
There are all kinds of dreams.
There are good dreams,
funny and beautiful dreams.
And sometimes there are
very bad and scary dreams.
When Prudence has a good, funny,
and beautiful dream, she smiles
in her sleep and sometimes
even laughs out loud.

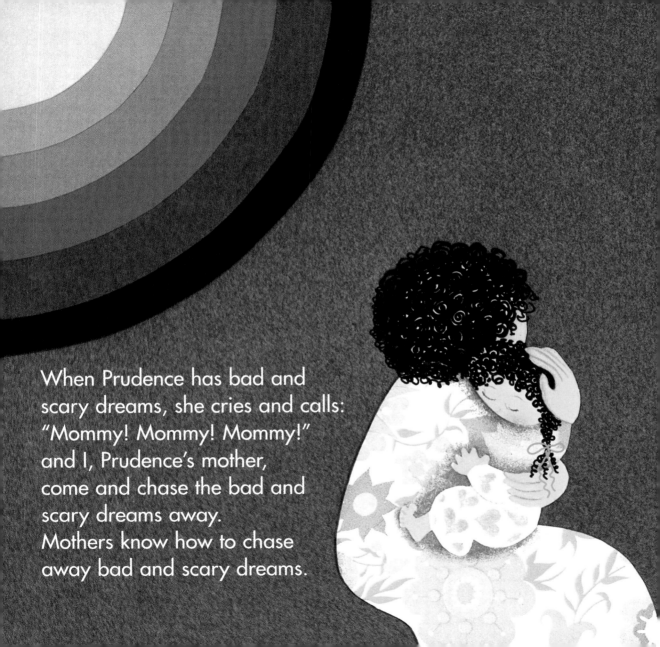

When Prudence has bad and
scary dreams, she cries and calls:
"Mommy! Mommy! Mommy!"
and I, Prudence's mother,
come and chase the bad and
scary dreams away.
Mothers know how to chase
away bad and scary dreams.

Prudence draws pictures of all kinds of dreams.
Every evening Prudence chooses a dream picture and
puts it under her pillow: The Travel Dream, The Rainbow Dream,
The Spring Dream, The Sun Dream, The Sea Dream.
Prudence also draws a magic picture that chases away bad
and scary dreams. When Prudence is afraid of having a bad
and scary dream she puts the magic picture under her pillow,
and all the bad and scary dreams go away.
Of course I, Prudence's mother, am always here to chase
away the bad and scary dreams if they come back.

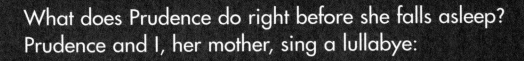
What does Prudence do right before she falls asleep?
Prudence and I, her mother, sing a lullabye:

The sun has gone to sleep
Hush . . . hush . . . hush . . .
Lovely sun
Hush . . . hush . . . hush . . .
Sleep sleep
All the trees have gone to sleep
Hush . . . hush . . . hush . . .
Rustling trees
Hush . . . hush . . . hush . . .
Sleep sleep
All the flowers have gone to sleep
Hush . . . hush . . . hush . . .

Beautiful flowers
Hush . . . hush . . . hush . . .
Sleep sleep
All the lions have gone to sleep
Hush . . . hush . . . hush . . .
Brave lions
Hush . . . hush . . . hush . . .
Sleep sleep*
Shhhh . . . Goodnight.

*Here you can continue endlessly or until one of you falls asleep.

Alona Frankel is the
author and illustrator of
over thirty titles for children,
including the well-known ONCE
UPON A POTTY. She is the recipient
of numerous awards, and her books
and art are seen all around the world.
Ms. Frankel lives in Tel Aviv, Israel.

Find out more about Alona
Frankel on the internet at:
www.alonafrankel.com